Return to Songbird Cottage (Pleasant Bay Book 2)

Sylvia Price

Penn and Ink Writing, LLC

Stay Up to Date with Sylvia Price

Subscribe to Sylvia's newsletter at newsletter.sylviaprice.com to get to know Sylvia and her family. It's also a great way to stay in the loop about new releases, freebies, promos, and more.

As a thank-you, you will receive a FREE exclusive short story that isn't available for purchase.

Praise for Sylvia Price's Books

"Wow, what a great start to a new series, and I really enjoyed reading it as it was so well-written, and I can't wait to read the next book. This is the first book that I have read by Sylvia Price but not the last and I recommend you read it and you will not be disappointed."

"Author Sylvia Price wrote a storyline that enthralled me. The characters are unique in their own way, which made it more interesting. I highly recommend reading this book. I'll be reading more of Author Sylvia Price's books."

"I love the way this is a very real example of one of the beauties of these small towns! Of course, mixing in beautiful scenery and the growing love with an old friend makes this the perfect start to a new series!"

"I've read several books written by Sylvia Price; she has done a great job at writing a good short story; she is becoming one of my favorite authors. I can't wait to read more of books her books."

"The storyline caught my attention from the very beginning and kept me interested throughout the entire book. I loved the chemistry between the characters."

"The plot flows easily, and the characters are appealing. It's a great story that shows what is most important in life."

"A wonderful, sweet and clean story with strong characters. Now I just need to know what happens next!"

"I just could not put this book down. Thank you for a delightful read."

"I love Sylvia's books because they are filled with love and faith."

"Sylvia's books ooze with love and goodness."

Other Books by Sylvia Price

Jonah's Redemption: Book 1 – FREE

Jonah's Redemption: Book 2 – Available on Amazon

Jonah's Redemption: Book 3 – Available on Amazon

Jonah's Redemption: Book 4 – Available on Amazon

Jonah's Redemption: Book 5 – Available on Amazon

Jonah's Redemption: Boxed Set – Available on Amazon

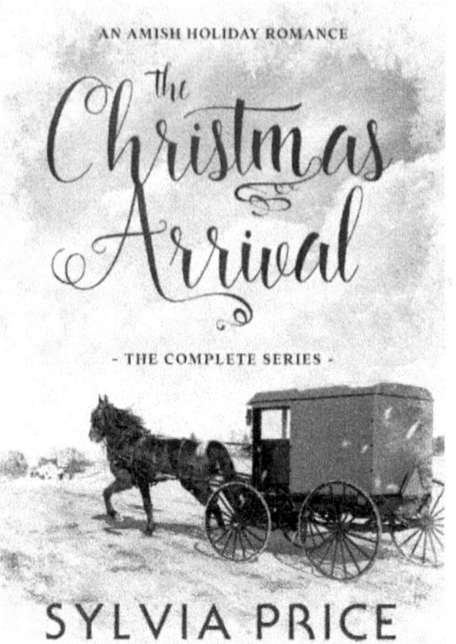# *The Christmas Arrival* – Available on Amazon

Contents

Chapter One: Fresh Starts and New Beginnings

The stones on the driveway gave their familiar crackle, alerting Emma that someone was approaching. Visitors were always a welcome break to an otherwise very predictable routine, and Emma moved to switch on the kettle before even checking to see who was walking towards the cottage.

Springtime at Songbird Cottage was just as delightful as the previous two seasons had been. Fall had brought golden leafy canopies of splendor; winter had been crisp and biting enough to remind Emma she was warm and alive.

Her second husband, Andrew's, death the previous year and the discovery that he had left her emotionally and financially bankrupt seemed like a distant memory to Emma now. Her retreat to Songbird Cottage at the beginning of fall had only been possible by the kindness extended to her by her first husband, John. He had invited her to make his sweet, little holiday cottage at Pleasant Bay on Cape Breton Island her new home.

Her website design company had been a success for both Emma and the happy local business owners who needed to update their online profiles. Filled with confidence after becoming a productive member of this beloved community, Emma had been able to put aside her anger and despair and start her life anew at the age of fifty-one. It hadn't hurt having neighbor Sam there by her side, ready to comfort Emma whenever he came over. That had really helped heal her issues with trust, in addition to keeping her cozy over winter!

Emma smiled to herself as she remembered the winter evenings with Sam by her side—the fires, the hot meals, and the peace and security of knowing they could laze on the couch together, reading the latest novel or watching a movie. Only someone who had figuratively had the carpet ripped out from under her feet could understand the immense appeal of stability and love as Emma could.

When a knock sounded, Emma went to open the door. Standing on the welcome mat outside the threshold was one of her favorite clients, a lawyer from Sydney named Kate Pfeiffer.

"Did you get my text?" Kate got straight to the point. "I sent it during the Englishtown to Jersey Cove ferry crossing."

"C'mon in, Kate." Emma opened the door wider and then stepped over to the battered old dining table where she kept her phone plugged into the back of her laptop to charge. She unplugged the phone and held it up to check the message icons.

"Whoops. Sorry. I forgot to switch off the Do Not Disturb settings this morning."

Kate smiled forgivingly. "With anyone else, I would've been worried and called before arriving. But you're always here, Emma, so I came over anyway. The drive from Sydney to Pleasant Bay is so beautiful; I don't know how you can concentrate on work when you could be out hiking or something."

Emma poured her visitor a mug of coffee and added a dash of cream the way she knew Kate liked it. As she handed it to Kate,

Emma motioned with her hand to the tin of cookies that sat open on the work desk. Kate smiled, selected a cookie, and then nibbled it before starting to explain the reason for her visit.

"I've decided to take on a new associate partner to share the workload," Kate informed Emma in between nibbles. "I've brought a USB flash drive with me. It has all his details on it, you know—credentials, professional pic *with a smile*—the same way you asked me to change mine, and then I need you to add a "Tax" section and an "Energy" section as well. My new partner brings with him an intimate knowledge of green energy projects and tax laws and regulations. He's just who I need to round off the services I already provide."

Emma extended her hand for the flash drive and popped it into the back of her laptop after Kate placed it in her palm. They both waited for the computer to recognize the device, and when the small arrow labeled "Richard Benson" appeared in the window, Emma clicked on it while taking a small sip of coffee.

"Whoa, Kate! Are you sure you aren't starting up a modeling agency instead of a law firm?" Emma asked when the image of Richard Benson came up on the screen.

"I know," Kate sighed. "He *is* very good looking, isn't he? But I am way past the age of falling in love with a pretty face, Emma, and he is exceptionally well-qualified."

Emma laughed, and Kate joined in with a sheepish giggle.

"Two middle-aged ladies goggling over a handsome face." Emma chuckled. "Is he single? Or are you hoping to get all the old biddies in Sydney to come over and ask him to help them with their wills?"

"He's single, actually a local boy who went across to the mainland to attend law school there. His mother is sick—one of those awful early-onset dementia cases—and his father needs all the help he can get, so Richard came back to Cape Breton to support them."

"How kind," Emma said, as she gave the words on the flash drive a quick read-through. "He sounds ideal for your firm, especially in the areas where he's specialized." Emma snapped her laptop lid closed. "I'll have a mock-up of the new pages ready for you by the weekend, Kate. Please tell your new partner I say hello and welcome back to Cape Breton. I wish it were under happier circumstances, but I'm sure it's a great comfort to his parents to have him home."

"Thanks, Emma," Kate responded as she moved towards the door. "I'm going to say hi to a few of my friends on this side of the island before driving back and maybe pick up a case of beers over at Sam's too. When are you two going to move in together? It's been six months now, and you're both not getting any younger."

Emma gave a small sigh as she walked with Kate to her car. "So many people have been asking that and probably thinking that as well. But it's not that simple on my side, Kate. My second husband died only last year. He was a real rat, but not everyone knows that. All they are going to see is a widow making merry with her neighbor."

Kate saw the worried frown on Emma's face and stopped looking for the car keys in her purse.

"Surely that shouldn't be a problem, Emma. I can vouch for all the folks around here. All we want is to see you settled, and Sam too."

Emma gave a small smile. "That's very sweet of you to say, Kate, but I hate the thought of shacking up with a man at my age, and it's too soon to be talking about a *third* marriage!"

Kate gave a pantomime grimace when Emma said the word, "marriage" and replied, "I see so many couples come in for pre-nups, but even more come to see me when they want to separate and don't have them!"

Kate hopped into her car, gave Emma a cheery wave, and drove away slowly. Sam's brewery was less than 150 yards down the road, and Emma knew he was there because the smell of coffee being roasted over hot coals was floating over the treetops.

Maybe I am being stubborn about moving in with Sam. We have spoken about what to do when my lease runs out here. Should I bring the subject up again when he visits tonight?

There was no chance of Sam moving in with Emma or them both finding someplace new. Sam's brewery was his passion, and he often spoke about passing it on to one of his sons if they decided to move back to Cape Breton. Sam had recently expanded the premises as the demand grew for his beer. Each batch was brewed using water straight from the Grande Anse River and locally produced ingredients. At the beginning of the year, he had added cold brew coffee, home-roasted coffee beans, and apple jelly to his product list. Emma had updated his website so customers could order everything online. Packing and shipping kept Sam so busy over weekends that he was thinking about hiring a student to help him out over the summer.

There's no way Sam would leave his brewery, but I've come to love Songbird Cottage so much. It always reminds me of how lucky I am to get another chance at love.

Emma stretched her legs with a walk around Songbird Cottage's garden. The rosebushes were pushing out new shoots, and the bulbs she had planted in winter were starting to poke their chartreuse-colored heads out of the rich, dark soil. Emma would bend down occasionally to tug out a weed or pick up an old empty seed packet that the wind had blown across the lawn.

Spring always brought with it the possibility of fresh starts and new beginnings. The smell of soil from her garden beds was husky and earthy. Emma inhaled deeply, caught the scent of roasting coffee beans with her breath, and was inspired to go back inside for something to drink.

Just as Emma got to her desk, the phone rang. She picked it up to check if she recognized the caller before answering. The screen showed that it was John.

John Havisham had been teenage Emma's first love. They had been amicably divorced now for over twenty-five years. Even though he had been considered one of the finest medical clinic property developers on the east coast, John had left New York at the first opportunity and moved to Nova Scotia.

A medical doctor, John had fallen in love with the province of Nova Scotia after spending two weeks of his precious vacation time there about twenty years ago. After marrying his long-time girlfriend, a seductive florist named Linette, John had found her obsession with climbing up the Manhattan social scene to be as boring and hollow as Linette had found it fulfilling.

Despite Linette's complaints and protests, John had sold off a large percentage of his properties and relocated to Halifax after finding a sprawling mansion sitting on the Northwest Arm with its own jetty and seventy yards of docking space. He had brought his parents with him and installed them at the closest nursing home. When they had passed away, he bought a bigger boat and took lessons on how to sail and navigate. After a lifetime of caring for others, John wanted to spend a little time devoted to his own leisure and pursuits.

A drunk driver had nearly upset John's plans for semi-retirement and more time for outdoor activities last year. John's car had been driven off the road and smashed into a wall. It was a miracle he had survived, but thanks to the staff at the QEII hospital in Halifax, not only had John survived, but he'd made a full recovery. Emma was always glad to have a chat with her ex-husband. Having two beautiful daughters together had ensured that communication between them had not just remained cordial, but encouragingly close as well.

"Hey there," Emma said when she answered John's call. "How're things on your side? How's Izzy." Their youngest daughter, Isabelle, had been staying with her father since his accident. She was very close to her father and couldn't rest easy in New York until he was back on his feet.

"Hey, Emma." John sounded tired and business-like. Emma hoped he didn't have bad news about her having to move out of Songbird Cottage again. Linette had tried to force her out when John had been unconscious in the hospital. Emma had had to hire Kate to defend her rights and fight the eviction. Kate had assured her that the lease agreement ensured that Emma could sit tight in Pleasant Bay for the next ten years if that's what she wanted.

Emma heard John exhale loudly into the phone, and then he said, "Linette and I are getting a divorce. I was wondering if I could come and stay with you for a while."

Chapter Two: Troubled Territory

Emma did not react immediately to what John had just told her. Every time John and Linette fought, he would call up Emma and tell her he was divorcing Linette. She thought it might be cathartic for him to do this every so often—a way of flexing his mental and emotional muscles in an attempt to give the problems in the relationship a workout.

What did make Emma's breath catch in her throat was the fact that John wanted to come and stay with her at Songbird Cottage. That statement definitely had to be clarified!

"I'm sorry to hear you're having trouble again, John." Emma tried hard to stop herself from stressing the word "again." Linette was a notoriously difficult person to get on with, but Emma believed that John had made his bed, so he should learn to lie on it.

"Troubles!" John's voice sounded outraged. "Troubles? My marriage moved from being in "troubles" territory and into complete collapse when I was unconscious, and my wife tried to have my daughter's credit cards suspended!"

Linette had gone power-mad when she had been left in charge of John's affairs after his accident. Besides trying to get Emma kicked out of Songbird Cottage a mere twelve hours after discovering John was in a coma, Linette had threatened Izzy too.

Isabelle "Izzy" Havisham was a free spirit who was still in the process of discovering what her true path was in life. She thought she may as well do it in New York as in any other place, and besides, it was easier to hook up with bandmates there. When she wasn't having online discussions about the pros and cons of drum machines or rehearsing, Izzy worked hard as a delivery person. The money she made doing that wasn't quite enough to support a busy Manhattan lifestyle, but her father had been more than happy to help out by providing her with a no-limit credit card, which he would pay off at the end of every month.

"It must've been a shock for you to find out about that." Emma always had to speak like a diplomat whenever John and Linette experienced one of their occasional breakups. She had learned the hard way that if she said anything disparaging about Linette or even agreed with John during these spats, he would resent her for it when the couple got back together.

"I'm through with being shocked about anything nasty when it comes to Linette right now, Emma." John's voice was so close to the phone that his words were echoing loudly into Emma's ear. She moved her device slightly away and pushed the speaker icon.

"Her actions were misguided; however, it's more important for you to find out the reasoning behind her thinking. Flight is not the answer, John. You should stay there and fight for your marriage. Go to counseling or convince her to see a psychiatrist—find out what it is that makes her hate your children so much."

Privately, Emma thought Linette needed an exorcist, not a psychiatrist, but she kept this to herself.

"Have you got me on speaker? I hope you're alone," John said, and this time his voice was pitched lower.

Emma reassured John. "We're alone; no one's listening. As I was saying, get her to a shrink. And force her creepy sons to go with her. I think they had a hand in pushing Linette to act the way she did."

"Forget Linette, and forget her two horrible sons, too." John was in no mood to be mollified or sidetracked. "Izzy says we should take the boat up to Sydney and then hire a car to drive us to Songbird Cottage. I need to get away from all this nonsense, and I can't think of a better place to do it than Pleasant Bay."

Emma tried to persist in discouraging John but was thrilled at the chance of seeing her daughter again. "It's very cramped and untidy here, you know. Perhaps you should stay in Sydney?"

"We'll work something out when we get there, Emma. See you soon."

The phone went dead. Emma felt slightly drained from her short conversation. John could be very forceful and abrupt when he wanted to be. It came from years of practice having to diagnose patients who didn't want to listen to the advice he was giving them. Emma wasn't quite sure she wanted to listen to John's problems, but there was a reason why she really had to give him the benefit of the doubt this time.

Since finding out she had no money left after Andrew died, Emma had come to value things she didn't realize were that important. A few undeniable facts had become clear to her as she struggled to restart her life. The first was that happiness was a state of mind and had nothing to do with money. The second was that having family and friends could only help up to a point, and then it was an individual choice to make the most of any advantages and blessings.

Emma understood how difficult it had been to count her blessings when it felt like the world was crashing down around her head, and she had Sam to thank for giving her the wake-up call she needed to have the depression-tinted scales fall from her eyes.

Thinking of Sam made Emma glance at her phone to check the time. Every evening, like clockwork, Sam would come over, and they would have a light supper together. Spring had brought with it a taste for less carb-heavy meals, and Emma wanted to make the drive over to Pleasant Bay to check out spring vegetables. She may as well stock up the kitchen in preparation for John and Izzy's visit while she was there.

First, Emma did all the housework she had been putting off for so long. With visitors on the way, it was time to do all the yucky chores that went over and beyond general household maintenance: cleaning the drains, dusting the tops of highly stacked bookcases and ledges, vacuuming the rugs, scrubbing the sink and bathroom floor. By the time she had finished, Emma's knees were shaking, and her elbows ached. She gave one last look around the cottage to make sure that she hadn't forgotten a corner or shelf, and then went out to her car, feeling very satisfied with Songbird Cottage's appearance. John wouldn't be able to say she wasn't looking after the place.

The drive into Pleasant Bay was always a delight. Emma never knew what view to expect when the road curved around to reveal the sea. Sometimes it was overcast and mournfully muted, sometimes it was mysteriously foggy, but most of the time, it was clear, blue, and speckled with sunrays bouncing off the waves. It never failed to give her spirits a lift.

Emma parked outside the general store that stocked all the basics she needed to buy. She had created websites for most of the shop owners in Pleasant Bay and also ran a local news blog about upcoming events, so she knew more about each little shop than any casual passerby. As she looked for a shopping cart, Emma was interrupted by one of her clients, Moira. She and her husband, Mike, owned and operated a bed and breakfast establishment just up the road.

"Hiya, Emma." Moira sounded cheerful. "How're things? Found any more antiques at the cottage, hey?" This was a long-standing joke between Emma and Moira.

Last year, when Linette had been in the process of evicting Emma from Songbird Cottage, a strange clause in John's living will had changed the course of her life forever. After offering Emma the cottage as a place to stay while she got her life back together, John had added a proviso to his power of attorney. It stated that while Linette owned and managed the summer cottage, Emma was the legal owner of everything inside it. Moira, a keen antique's collector and dealer, had discovered an extremely rare (and valuable) Cadwalader hairy paw chair among the old furniture and knickknacks there. Selling the chair had put Emma back on her feet financially.

I must remember to thank John for his kindness and forethought in arranging things the way he did. He must've had some premonition that Linette might take any chance she could to get me out of her life forever.

"I'm good, thanks, Moira. How are you and Mike? Things must be getting busy now that spring is well underway," was all Emma said out loud.

"That's true," Moira agreed. "No small thanks to you for up-dating our website, though. We're getting a lot of inquiries from it."

The two women moved up and down the aisles together, chatting and placing products and food items into their carts.

Moira gave Emma a recipe to make a light springtime quiche and helped her find the ingredients for it. Soon, Emma's cart was piled high with eggs, cream, asparagus, and shelled peas.

"I'm not sure if it freezes well," Moira said as she packed her groceries into the trunk of her car. "Let me know if it does because I would love to make more of these while spring veggies are so cheap."

"I will. Thank you. See you soon." Emma gave Moira a wave as she backed up her vehicle and drove off. She returned to placing her grocery bags into the hatchback's trunk and then got into the driver's seat. Car ownership was something Emma would never take for granted again, and she still treated her tiny compact car with respect.

After a quick glance right and left, Emma turned left back onto Cabot Trail and then immediately swung right towards Pleasant Bay Road. Her mind was occupied with how long it would take to bake the quiche before Sam joined her. The housework had taken longer than she had predicted, and Emma felt her quiche making skills were a little rusty. Also, she wasn't quite sure about baking times.

Emma almost thought she was hallucinating when she saw Chip drive past her. Her mind refused to process the image of Linette's youngest son's balding head, receding jaw, and rounded shoulders as his vehicle cruised past her at a leisurely pace. She fought the urge to whip her head around for a second look as the hatchback was approaching a corner. By the time she had made sure of her car's position on the road, it was too late to find out if the man really was Chip.

But it had been Chip; it was definitely him! I would recognize that fool's profile anywhere. What on earth is he doing here? Or was it some poor soul who just looks like him?

The rest of Emma's trip home was ruined by fruitless speculation and conjecture. Sure, it might have been someone who looked like him, and Chip was miles away in Halifax anyway. The way that driver was hunched over the steering wheel was uncannily similar to the way Chip sat. But what reason would he have to be here? The endless questions went around and around in her head, and Emma drove up to Songbird Cottage with no clear idea of how she felt about the man who looked like Chip.

Sam was waiting for her inside. He looked up as Emma came in.

"What's up, Em?" he asked. "You look like you've seen a ghost."

Chapter Three: I Saw a Man Who Wasn't There

"I saw a man who wasn't there, or wasn't meant to be here, at any rate," Emma said as she plonked the bags down on her workbench.

"What are you talking about?" Sam asked as he got up to help Emma put away the groceries. She made a shooing gesture with her hand, saying, "No, let me do this. If you help me, it only ends up with me walking around in circles later on when I can't figure out where something is."

Sam contentedly sat back down on the old velvet couch in the living area. "You were about to tell me about the man who wasn't there," he reminded Emma.

"Oh, you know that poem they used to teach in schools. 'I saw a man on the stairs who wasn't there'—I can't remember who wrote it—but it ends with the poet writing 'I wish, I wish he wasn't there?' Well, that's exactly how I feel right now."

"You're talking about 'Antigonish,' you mean?" Sam said. "I loved that poem when I was a kid—spooky, yet kind of quirky."

"Yep. It always gave me the shivers when I was young—the thought of a thing on the stairs that may or may not be real. I had the strangest fleeting glimpse, just now on the drive home, of a man who looked like Linette's son, Chip. But it couldn't have been him. It would take a giant-sized boot kicking his bum for him to leave his precious gaming console in Halifax."

Sam rolled his eyes so hard Emma could see him do it, even though she was standing on the other side of the room. "He sounds like a real loser," Sam said with a frown. "How old are her sons? Aren't they around the same age as your two girls?"

"Close enough," Emma replied. "Her youngest son, Chip—the one I thought I saw—is about Claire's age, so say thirty-one or thereabouts. And her eldest boy, Chuck, is about four or five years older. I used to feel sorry for them both when they were growing up because their father remarried and moved to Ghana when they were still children. He lost contact with them when his second batch of kids came along. That might have had something to do with wanting to disassociate himself from Linette though."

"Can't blame him for wanting to do that," Sam said, "but deadbeat dads are all scoundrels, no matter what the circumstances are."

"I'm sure he didn't feel like he was truly abandoning them, Sam, because Linette had hooked up with John by then, and even though they weren't officially together, John was still paying for everything—kids included."

"How noble of him," was all Sam said.

"Hang on a minute," Emma shouted over the scream of the hand mixer. "I have to whip the eggs and cream for the quiche."

When the sound of the hand mixer stopped, Sam was checking his phone for messages and texting back replies. Emma saw her opportunity.

"Speaking of John," she began, "I got a phone call from him today." Emma tried to sound nonchalant.

Sam's head snapped up, and he put his phone down.

"Really? How is the poor old guy doing?"

"I didn't get a chance to ask. He got straight to the point and said that he's divorcing Linette. Izzy and John are sailing up the coast to Sydney tomorrow and then driving around to Pleasant Bay." Emma looked down to concentrate on her quiche pastry.

"Where will they be staying?" Sam was full of questions tonight, and who could blame him?

"I'm not sure yet." Emma wasn't entirely certain if she should disclose John's plan to Sam or not, so she decided against it. "But they will be here within the next few days because John says he needs Pleasant Bay to soothe his jangled nerves."

"He's definitely coming to the right place then." Sam smiled across at Emma and then looked back down at his phone.

Emma couldn't help feeling a wave of relief that Sam had taken the news so well. She felt grateful that he had such a calm manner. Sam was a man of few words but was always ready to leap into action when it counted. Emma placed the quiche gently onto the rack in the middle of the oven and carefully poured in the cream and egg mixture. She closed the oven door, set the timer for thirty minutes, and walked over to where Sam was sitting.

"Thank you for being so understanding," Emma said as she sat down next to Sam on the low sprung velvet couch. "I bet John goes back to Linette after one or two weeks. That's what he's always done before. As soon as he gets to the part where the lawyers start talking about a division of assets, he backs down and decides it's better for his bank account to stick it out."

Sam inclined his head towards Emma so that he could look at her without hurting his neck. "Why didn't he ever have another affair? He was quick enough to cheat on you, wasn't he? Not to judge him or her, but he seems like the kind of guy who wouldn't bat an eyelid about sleeping around, and she seems like the type of wife who would be happy turning a blind eye just so long as she has her credit cards."

Emma smiled and then sighed. "He had the odd fling with other women in his younger days, but he's petrified of being baby-trapped now. He's in his mid-sixties, y'know, and his biggest fear is that a lady-friend might 'accidentally' get pregnant."

Sam grunted when he heard this and put his arm around the back of the couch to hug Emma closer, saying, "He sounds like he's got a few things to sort out in his life, and getting a divorce might only be one of them." Sam leaned over, found the computer mouse, and activated the play button on their favorite streaming channel. "I guess he's coming to the perfect place in which to do it."

∞ ∞ ∞

Sam left bright and early the next day to get a head start on packing and shipping his online orders. Sometimes Emma would go and help him, but she also had work to do today. Kate's new law partner's profile had to be loaded onto the site.

Emma spent the morning creating URL links and metadata. It was a tedious task and one which she was very happy to be able to put behind her when the clock on the laptop told her it was time for lunch. Emma pushed her chair back from the desk, stretched, and then walked over to the kitchenette. She thought about reheating some quiche and maybe making a salad to go with it.

There's no way I'm going to reheat the quiche in the microwave. That's sure to make the pastry soggy. I think I'll take a stroll around the garden to check on the pruning while the slice heats up in the oven.

Emma loved to walk around Songbird Cottage's garden. No matter what season this beautiful space experienced, there was always something interesting happening with the plants and trees. In winter, it had been fun to scrape the snow off the ground and trees to see what was happening underneath, but now it was spring, and things were really starting to kick into gear. The half-acre of land the cottage stood on was a labyrinth of rose beds, fruit trees, and creeping ground cover. Sometimes, she had to look closely at the foliage to see if a plant was still healthy, and Emma found that strolling up and down doing this was a great way to break up the day.

While inspecting her garden, Emma took in a deep breath, held it for a few seconds, and then exhaled forcefully out of her mouth. There must have been some pollen or dust in the crisp air because Emma sneezed. She felt around in her pockets for a tissue and then decided to go back inside and use a fresh one. Walking slowly down the gentle slope that tilted the pathway towards the front door, something caught the side of her eye.

Thinking it must be an illusion caused by the angle and direction of the driveway, Emma trotted quickly down to where her beloved little hatchback stood parked. She would have been sure right away if her car had been an SUV, but her diminutive vehicle's tires were small to suit the rest of the car. When she got close enough, Emma bent down and peered at the tires more attentively.

Both of the tires on the left-hand side of the hatchback had been slashed. There was no doubt about it. Huge gashes punctured the side of the rubber, leaving the tire walls resembling a donut with sprinkles. Panicked, Emma darted around to the other side of the car. The other two tires had also been hacked with some sort of stabbing instrument. Without even being aware of it, Emma stood up and looked around. Suddenly Songbird Cottage didn't feel peaceful and safe anymore.

Who could have been so mean as to do this?

Emma cast her mind back into the recent past but could find no reason for a local person to get this angry with her. In fact, it had been quite the opposite. From the time she had moved back to Pleasant Bay, Emma knew her life had been made richer by the people who lived here. The whole island seemed to be a place where folks had access to some hidden well of contentment that wasn't available anywhere else. If one of her clients hadn't been quite satisfied with their website, they would simply pick up the phone and tell her.

Sam's ex-wife was fortunately remarried to a farmer in South Africa, and his three sons were pleased their father had finally settled down with the woman for whom he'd been carrying a torch these past twenty years.

It can't be anyone I know, surely, could it?

Unsure of what to do but realizing her afternoon would be spent on the phone getting quotes for tires and car service fees, Emma pushed Sam's number.

"Yep." Sam answered the phone the way he lived his life: direct and to the point.

"Sam," Emma uttered, hoping her voice didn't sound as hysterical and worried as she was actually feeling, but there was still a bit of a waver in it. "Someone has slashed all the tires on my precious little hatchback." Her voice broke when she said this, and genuine distress overwhelmed her. "Please come over. I'm not sure how to handle this."

"Be there soon," Sam said and hung up the phone.

Emma waited in the driveway for Sam's SUV to drive up. Within a few minutes, she heard the sound of a car engine and walked down to the bottom of the property to watch his approach. For some reason, Emma didn't feel comfortable about going back inside the cottage until Sam was with her.

The car pulled up to the curb, and Sam got out. He looked calm, but the set of his mouth was a little grim. He took Emma by the hand and walked with her towards the hatchback. From the back, the little car looked listless and broken. One side tilted lower than the other, and the back bumper had nearly settled on the ground on the right side.

Sam put his hand on the car roof and gave it a pat. Then he walked all the way around it, bending over at each corner to inspect the wheels more closely. When he returned to where Emma was standing, he gave her a hug. He understood how much the car meant to Emma. When she had first arrived on the island, she had no longer owned a vehicle since her convertible had been repossessed. After selling the Cadwalader chair, the hatchback was the first thing she'd bought. It signified freedom, success, and hope to Emma. Now, it had been temporarily ruined.

Sam patted Emma's back a few times to comfort her before he pulled away and looked at her face.

"No permanent harm done, Em. I'll give my mechanic a call, and he'll take care of it."

Emma felt relief wash over her like a warm shower. She gave a doleful sniff, and they both turned to walk back to the cottage.

Sam held Emma's hand as they went back up the driveway.

"Well," he said, "I guess we can be sure of one thing. That was most definitely Chip you saw on Pleasant Bay Road."

Chapter Four: The Arrival

A few days later in the week, Emma's peace and quiet was rudely interrupted by the sound of a loud horn blaring outside the cottage's windows. She jumped in her seat and strode to the front door in anticipation of her youngest daughter running in to greet her.

When no one burst in, Emma opened the door and peered outside to see what was delaying Izzy's excited hug. Her mouth dropped open in shock when she saw a motorhome as big as a cruise ship parked a couple of yards away.

The RV was massive enough to cause Emma to have to tilt her head up so as to see it in full. Not only was the motorhome multi-level, but it seemed to have space underneath the floorboards too. Emma hoped it didn't hold a cellar full of jet skis in there. She looked up at the driver's area and caught her first glimpse of John. He looked exhilarated at having caused such a commotion. One side of his hair was still growing back since being shaved off after the accident, but he was still recognizably himself. Izzy was gesticulating wildly beside him, pointing behind and above her, and then all around.

Emma gave a feeble wave and waited patiently for Izzy to work out how to lower the stairway down to ground level.

"Isn't this the best!" Izzy shouted to her mother after jumping off the last step. "Dad ordered it to be delivered to the Sydney docks! We disembarked from *The Radium*, and it was waiting for us right there. There was a huge crowd of people standing around it. They all thought it might belong to a rock band or something. Dad says I can borrow it to tour in when my band makes it big. How are you?"

Izzy was too busy supplying her mother with information about the motorhome to notice her less than enthusiastic appraisal of the vehicle.

Emma returned her daughter's hug and then began talking to John as he approached. "When are you going to embrace the new attitude to consumerism and buy something more compact?" She leaned forward to give her ex-husband a hug and then smiled.

John grinned. "It's awesome, isn't it? I have this great idea to paint the bodywork with something outrageous, just to see people's faces when we drive by."

"When *you* drive by, you mean," Emma replied. "I wouldn't be caught dead in one of those gas guzzlers."

Izzy and John both made noises that signified disagreement. Izzy began to recite a catalog of the motorhome's advantages as she linked her arm through Emma's and began to guide her inside towards the kettle.

"It's diesel, so it gets more miles to the gallon. It's more cost-efficient and greener than staying in a hotel. And the best thing is that Dad can live at the bottom of the garden, and you won't even know he's there."

"If you think buying an RV that clearly cost upwards of six figures is cheaper than Pleasant Bay accommodations, you clearly don't know how reasonably priced the bed and breakfasts are round here," Emma replied as she poured boiling water into a teapot.

"Oh Mom, just be grateful Dad's not sleeping in Claire's bed in the guestroom. I don't know why, but he really wants to be here for some reason. Pleasant Bay has meant a lot to him since he bought the cottage." Here Izzy lowered her voice, checked over her shoulder to see if John was still offloading their baggage, then turned back to Emma, whispering, "He's brought Granny and Grandpa's ashes—he wants to scatter them here, or something— just be *kind*. He's been through a lot."

They heard John come in the door, banging the backpack he was carrying against the doorframe. Emma didn't reply to what Izzy had told her. She nodded her head to show her daughter she understood, and then went to help John with Izzy's luggage.

Getting settled in the cottage didn't take Izzy long. She planned on doing some hiking and backpacking while she was here, and most of the stuff she had brought with her could fit inside her enormous hiking backpack. Emma asked her curiously if she had enough outfits to last through her stay.

"You seem to have only brought hiking boots and hi vis jackets with you, Izz."

"If I run out of something, I can always drive across to Sydney and buy it there," she responded casually. Emma, still pinching pennies after Andrew had left her bankrupt, couldn't help but wish she had her daughter's indifferent attitude towards spending, which she could afford to have since John was still paying Izzy's credit card bills.

John came back inside with a trash bag full of junk food wrappers and empty soda bottles. "Where's your recycling bin?" he asked Emma.

"You never ordered one for the cottage, and I haven't gotten around to doing it either, so I just take my bags into town and sort my recycling there."

"Fair enough," John replied cheerfully as he went back outside to the trash can.

"He seems to have mellowed quite a bit since the accident," Emma said quietly to Izzy. Her daughter was sifting through the items in her bag and only grunted as a reply. She must have found what she was searching for because Izzy sat up, waving her toiletry kit in the air.

"I'm off to the bathroom to brush my teeth. I ate so much candy on the road, my teeth feel as though they're coated in fur."

Emma was left in the cottage with John.

Now is the time to thank him for giving me the furniture and the million-dollar chair.

John was pouring himself a cup of tea. "Got any skimmed milk?" he asked Emma as he opened the fridge.

"Nope, sorry. John, I'm glad I have a moment to talk to you about the chair. You probably know it saved me a lot of tears and drama when you organized things that way. I don't know if I can ever thank you enough. It's not as though you didn't sort things out fairly after our divorce; it's just that Andrew left me with nothing, and then Linette wanted to evict me from the cottage. The money from selling the chair got me out of that hole, but I still have most of the money from the auctioneer in my account. I used a bit for the car and to upgrade the windows of the cottage for winter. I had to pay cash because my credit score is in the toilet since the bankruptcy. You can have the rest if you want."

John sat down in one of the dining chairs next to Emma's laptop.

"Don't worry about it. I had a feeling when you moved up here that Linette," he said the name with a grimace of distaste on his face, "would try to ruin your life if anything happened to me. It wasn't enough for her that Andrew blew all your money and savings, oh no. She said you deserved to be ruined."

Emma closed her eyes as though she were in acute pain. Linette had the power to make someone experience extremely vengeful thoughts.

"I tried changing things around in my living will, will, power of attorney, you name it. But my lawyer said that if I made it obvious that I was giving you money, Linette would simply go to court and freeze things up with an injunction. I knew she didn't know about my mother's Cadwalader chair and figured out that was the best way I could give you money if anything happened to me. She would've been fine with you having all Songbird Cottage's contents. She hasn't got a clue about antiques because she's always hired interior decorators to do our homes with the latest modern furnishings."

John stopped talking. He sighed and looked around the cottage. "I've always loved this place. It's hauntingly lovely without being haunted. It's restful without being boring. Time seems frozen here."

"I get what you mean," Emma said as she sipped on her tea. "Songbird Cottage has a way of healing a person, and I guarantee you'll feel more optimistic in a few days' time." Emma looked more keenly at her ex-husband. He had his head thrown back, and he was staring blissfully up at the cottage's exposed roof rafters. "How long do you plan on staying?"

John looked around and saw Izzy coming back up out of the sunken bathroom area underneath the mezzanine floor where Emma slept. "I don't know yet. I might join Isabelle on her Cabot

Trail trek or hang out in the RV—lie low for a bit after all the drama, trauma, hysteria…"

Izzy spoke out in agreement. "Yes! That old bat has been screaming at Dad non-stop since he gave Linette her marching orders. Good riddance to bad rubbish, that's what I say."

"Izzy!" Emma said in a shocked voice, but then she saw that John was nodding his head in agreement.

"My lawyer Gerald has retired, and he was no good at divorce settlements anyway. I'm going to need a killer attorney because Linette has her eldest son, Chuck, working around the clock on ways to screw me in the divorce settlement," John said matter-of-factly as he got up to return to his motorhome. "Come and see the RV, Emma. This beast is like a mobile penthouse suite. Even my bathroom is bigger than yours."

Emma walked out with John and Izzy to admire the vehicle. She mounted the stairs and entered the first level. John was in his element giving her a guided tour.

"It's made by the same designers in Florida who did Will Smith's "The Heat." What do you think of that?"

Emma knew nothing about RVs and even less about Will Smith and what kind of recreational vehicle he owned. "Wow, nice. So cool," was all she could think of to say as John ushered her up and down and all around.

The fittings and amenities were really something else. Even Emma couldn't help but be impressed with the long kitchenette down one side of the home and the cocktail drinking area opposite it.

"Watch this," John said as he held out a mobile console device in front of him. Emma felt a motor whir, and the kitchenette began to expand outwards and increase the floor space. The audio and video systems flickered to life, and LED lights twinkled above her like fairy dust.

"Did you custom order it or buy it off the shop floor?" Emma asked as she walked upstairs to the seating area. She saw there was a fireplace at one end and a master bedroom at the other. In between the two areas were luxurious recliners, widescreens, and end tables. She could see why Izzy would encourage her father to buy one of these things. She heard her daughter downstairs, playing a video game. The cottage was low on technology, and Emma wondered if the motorhome had its own Wi-Fi or if she should call her service provider to increase her bandwidth.

"We bought it off the shop floor after looking over the specs online. Izzy requested them to deliver the van to Sydney, so we were spared having to travel to Florida for pick-up."

John stroked the back of one of the cream-colored leather loungers affectionately, saying, "I'm never going back to Halifax, Emma. Or at least not until Linette has gone back to live in New York. Can you believe her father's still alive in a nursing home there?"

Emma couldn't help but look shocked at the news. "Her father must be over ninety years-old now, what with Linette approaching her seventies. How is the old man?"

John hated being reminded about his age. Even though it had been the thirteen-year age gap between himself and Emma that had driven them apart, he must have felt slightly snippy by Emma's referral to his wife's age, as Linette and John had been born in the same year.

"She's only sixty-four, Emma. Same as I am. Sheesh! You act as though I'm divorcing Linette because she's getting old. I'm not. I'm divorcing her because she's a creepy, embittered woman who acted in a completely unacceptable way towards my daughters when I was unconscious." John shut his mouth by pressing his lips together, but he couldn't stop himself from voicing his main suspicion. "In fact, I think she was hoping that I might not recover at all."

Emma patted John's arm comfortingly. "I'm so happy you're better, John," she said soothingly. "I have a client who specializes in divorce, contracts, prenups, and stuff. Can I contact her on your behalf and set up a meeting? She's back in Sydney."

John perked up at what Emma told him. "Yes, please. That would help me a lot."

As they began to walk down to the garden, Sam's SUV rolled up the driveway.

Emma turned to her ex-husband, and said, "John, you're just in time to meet my friend, Sam MacAuley. I know you two have met before and have chatted on the phone, but Sam and I…"

Chapter Five: Another Attack

The thing was, Emma had never explained how things stood between herself and Sam to her family. First, she had told herself that it was because the relationship was still in its early days. Then she convinced herself that no one in the family would be interested in the love life of a fifty-one-year-old widow.

The fact was, Emma felt that making a formal announcement to her daughters about being Sam's girlfriend was just too embarrassing. She thought stayovers and date nights should strictly be left to people under the age of fifty. Sam had told his sons about being in a committed relationship with Emma over Christmas. They had been together for three months by then, and every day seemed to make the bond that existed between them even stronger.

Even though Emma had been okay telling her girls about her "friend" Sam, that's all the description about him she had ever gotten around to providing. Izzy came to stand beside her mother and father when she saw Sam get out of his car and begin walking up the driveway with his strong, rangy stride. It was now or never.

Emma took a deep breath and said as casually as she was able, "Oh, you should both know that Sam and I have been together since last fall. I know it's so soon after Andrew, but…"

Izzy said, "We know, Mom. Claire told me that was probably what had happened when you didn't come to Halifax for Christmas."

John laughed. "There's no keeping secrets from you two girls."

Emma was relieved the news had broken so easily and went forward to greet Sam with a hug. "Hey, you," she said in a whisper, "prepare yourself for a motorhome tour."

Sam walked up to where Izzy and John stood and shook John warmly by the hand. "It's good to see you back on your feet, John," he said. "You made these two ladies very worried, and Claire as well."

He stepped back to take in the full view of the behemoth of a motorhome.

"Whew! She's a beaut. Please give me the grand tour, John."

The two men climbed the stairway back into the RV, with Sam asking eager questions about miles per gallon, square footage, and toy haulers.

Emma headed outside with Izzy and gave her daughter's shoulders a squeeze. "Come and help me build a fire. I got some fresh fish and want to cook them over hot coals," she explained.

"Yum, sure thing, Mom," Izzy said as they walked back to the cottage.

The rest of the evening was spent chatting harmoniously about recreational vehicles, antiques, and the proliferation of fake medical papers using biased data—three subjects about which John felt very strongly.

Sam rose from the dining table later, saying, "I should call it a night. Thank you for a lovely meal, Emma. And thanks for offering to do the washing up, Izzy."

"What?" Izzy shouted from the comfort of the velvet couch where she had collapsed after her second helping of fish steak and salad.

Emma laughed. "We can take the dishes outside and stack them in the motorhome's washer, Izz. Calm down."

"Tomorrow, I will show you how all the appliances work, and then we can eat in the RV from now on," John said, also pushing his chair back from the table with a satisfied heave.

"I'll walk you out to the car, Sam," Emma said.

Sam put his hand up. "No, Em. It's fine. I'll see you tomorrow. Thanks again for dinner." After giving Izzy and John a cheerful farewell wave, Sam was gone.

Emma braced herself.

"So, Mom," Izzy began, "when are you two getting married?"

John was fiddling with the laptop mouse to find something he wanted to watch on the streaming service, but Emma knew he was pricking up his ears to hear how she replied.

"I've just recovered from the worst second marriage in history, Izz. I'm not keen to step back into matrimony right away." Emma thought she sounded calm and pragmatic and was pleased with herself.

"Yeah, but this time, it would be with Sam. And he's an open book, besides being someone you've known since forever. C'mon, Mom. I can't have two single parents. That would be weird."

"I'm not single, Isabelle. Just not married. There's a difference." Emma struggled to keep her voice from betraying her hesitance.

"And I'm separated, soon to be divorced," said John from his perch on the couch. "There's a difference there, too."

"Okay, jeez. You two sound so adamant about your relationship statuses, and you're not even on social media," Izzy said. "I'm going back to the van to play my game."

Izzy slouched out, leaving Emma to scrape the dishes clean while John watched a sitcom on the laptop. He would break into laughter occasionally and take a chug of Sam's craft beer. Emma felt a sense of déjà vu. She could remember when she was married to John and the family would experience a peaceful lull after dinner but before bedtime. She had always described it as "The Golden Moment." No more coffee buzz or list checking to see if all the tasks and chores had been done, just a mellow feeling of fullness from good food and the pleasant anticipation of bed.

As Emma was wiping down her counters and packing away the cutlery, John flayed around on the low couch a bit before he managed to elevate himself up from its soft velvety clutches. When he had managed to stand up, he said, "Thanks, Emma. I'll finish this program on my device in the motorhome. Remember not to lock the door because Izzy wants to sleep in her room here. She says my snoring is too loud."

"Gotcha," Emma said. "Good night John, and thanks again."

John nodded and went outside.

Emma heard the sounds of the motorhome's stairs being lowered, folded her dishcloth, and then headed to the bathroom.

∞ ∞ ∞

Early in the morning, Emma was woken up by the sound of her phone ringing. She kept her phone on the end table next to the bed, like everyone else in the world, with the ringer on but notifications off in case one of the girls had an emergency.

Emma fumbled to find the phone, and when she raised the device off the table surface, the neon glow from the screen nearly blinded her eyes with its brightness.

"Wah?" Emma managed as she pushed the green answer icon.

"Help me, please!" It was John. "I think I've had a stroke!"

Emma sat up, turned on the light, and began looking for her robe. "You sound fine, John. Why do you think it's a stroke?"

"Hurry!" John screamed into the receiver. "Something's wrong, I tell you. I feel off-balance, and I think I'm hallucinating —just get in here, *please*! I can't remember where the light switch is."

Emma knew that John had been pessimistic about his health since he had been discharged from the hospital after the accident. The girls had told her he had been left with a generally bleak worldview, especially since finding out about Linette's behavior when she thought he would never regain consciousness. Emma understood everything there was to know about bleak world-views. Her heart went out to her ex-husband as she climbed down the mezzanine stairs and walked over to the drawer where she kept her flashlight.

After activating the light to its brightest setting, Emma walked outside. The songbirds were singing to each other in the trees, so she gauged the time to be about five in the morning. She shined the flashlight down the garden to where the motorhome had been set up close enough to feed off electricity from the cottage.

Something wasn't right.

The motorhome looked like a sickly brachiosaurus. It was listing heavily to one side, with the driver's area resembling someone who had had their expensive sunglasses knocked skew off their face.

At least John is all right. It must feel very strange inside with the floor tilted like that.

Emma saw the stairs were still down and ran up them nimbly, the flashlight showing her where to place her feet. It wasn't the easiest thing to do, and Emma was strongly reminded of that scene in the movie *Titanic*, when the ship was sinking.

"John? I'm here. It's going to take a minute to come up, but please don't worry. It's just the RV; it's not a stroke."

Emma heard shouts coming from above her as she mounted the circular stairwell. Bracing herself against the loungers that had been conveniently locked into place on the floor, Emma made her way slowly over to John's bedroom. She managed to slide the door open, and her flashlight showed John sitting as upright as he could in a large bed, his eyes wide and staring like an owl.

"Thank goodness!" he said when Emma moved the beam away from his face and shined it onto the opposite wall. "What on earth is going on? It feels as though the bed is trying to throw me against the headboard."

Emma moved to where John was clinging to the bed. "There's something wrong with the bus," she said comfortingly. "I think it's broken." She reached her arms around John's shoulders so that he could brace himself and stand up.

"It's not a bus. It's a motorhome," John insisted, his penchant for correct terminology not diminished in the least by his distress, "and it can't be broken—I just bought it."

Emma made soothing noises as the two of them lurched across the floor and back down the stairs together.

"We must look like a couple of drunken idiots," John commented as they fell out of the door and staggered for a few steps before regaining their balance. "Give me the flashlight."

Emma handed it to him, and John ran around to the place where the motorhome's bumper was nearly touching the ground on one side. In fact, the entire right side of the van was almost at ground level, while the left side was raised unnaturally high.

"Be careful!" Emma warned. "It looks like it might topple over completely."

A strangled shout of outrage could be heard from the other side of the van. Emma felt her way over to where John was standing. She was glad to see the sky was turning gray in the east and hoped daylight would bring some answers with it.

John was standing next to what was left of the motorhome's tires. They were completely flat on one side. The two tires at which Emma looked had the cartoon-like appearance of deflated balloons.

"My dually! My precious dually—both of them! And the tire in front as well! Who could have done this?" John's face had gone red with rage. Emma was able to see this because the sun was now peeking over the horizon. Rouge sun fingers poked through tree branches and between gaps in the hedge. A new day was beginning.

As the sky turned from gray to red, John and Emma stood side by side looking at what was left of the RV's wheels. The garden grew brighter, and the songbirds' whistles and chirps grew louder. Emma turned to see if the tires on the other side of the vehicle had been damaged. That was when they both saw huge scrape marks running up and down the motorhome's paintwork.

Emma shivered and wrapped her robe tighter around herself.

Chapter Six: Time to Solve the Mystery

Emma busied herself with making everyone coffee. It was an impossible task to do in the motorhome this morning. John, galvanized by the attack on his cherished motorhome, had spent the day calling the Royal Canadian Mounted Police in Chéticamp and then looking for the names of security firms online.

Emma felt as though the other shoe would drop only when Sam arrived. There was a cold feeling in the pit of Emma's stomach. She never thought it would be possible to feel the presence of something so malignant at Songbird Cottage and was only able to rationalize the feeling of fear away by remembering that that was how the vandal *wanted* her to feel.

I'm not going to give in to this fear and trepidation of being under attack. But when Sam arrives, it's time we had a good, long chat with John.

Emma went outside the minute she heard Sam arrive and found him at the RV, bending to inspect the damage.

"Little Chippie strikes again," he quipped. "What did the RCMP say?"

"Come inside, why don't you?" Emma said with a small smile

at Sam's description of Linette's son. "We need to tell John about what's going on. I haven't said anything yet because it'll be better if it comes from both of us." And by that, Emma meant that John would have to believe Sam because he had nothing invested in an accusation.

When they entered the cottage, Sam and Emma were greeted by the sight of John pacing from one side of the cottage to the other. He had his phone pressed against one ear and a cup of coffee in his hand. He was listening intently to what the person on the other end of the line was saying.

"Don't give John any more coffee, Em," Sam said with a grin.

"Uh-huh, uh-huh. Thank you, goodbye," John said, and then pressed the red icon.

John turned to greet Sam. "Who would've thought the Cape Breton police would be so quick to try and solve this nonsense?"

"We don't actually call them that here, John," Emma interjected.

"Mounties, RCMP, whatever. I live in Halifax, Emma; I know what they're called," John snapped. "They are sending someone over to take fingerprints and get a statement. That means the scoundrel who harmed my motorhome will face jail time when he's caught."

"Crime is so rare here that they must've been real excited to get a case," Sam presumed.

Izzy laughed when she heard that as she came out of the girls' small bedroom. "I can imagine them going full-CSI when they arrive." She giggled as she poured herself a cup of coffee from the big pot on the stovetop.

Sam and Emma looked at each other, and Sam made a motion with his head to show Emma that she should be the one to begin speaking first.

"John, Izz, there's something I need to tell you. It might be linked to what happened to the RV." Emma hoped she sounded more emphatic compared to how she felt inside. Wild accusations weren't her cup of tea, and if John took this the wrong way, it might cause friction between everyone. Songbird Cottage was too small to have a trio of adults at one another's throats.

Izzy and John looked intrigued. John went to sit down at the dining table and motioned for everyone to join him. When they had all pulled out a chair, Emma began to speak.

"Okay. Last week, I thought I saw Chip on Pleasant Bay Road. That night, the tires on my hatchback were slashed too. I think—"

"And so do I," Sam added.

"—that Chip is doing this," Emma finished.

Silence descended over the dining table. Izzy had her mouth open, and John's face was turning beet red. Emma didn't know whether he would explode in wrath at her, or not.

Izzy and John began talking all at once.

"That sneaky rat!"

"It's totally something he would do!"

"I'm going to strangle that no-good—"

"He's a malicious little weasel, Dad!"

Emma was relieved that they believed her. She hated the possibility of being thought of as a trouble-stirrer.

The red faded from John's face, and he grew calm. Years of discipline as a doctor kicked in, and his brain quickly began to formulate a strategy to combat the tactics being used against him.

"That's good to know, Emma. Thank you." John turned to Izzy and said, "Let's go to Sydney tomorrow and speak to the security provider based there. I'm going to catch that jerk red-handed. It's going to take an entire battalion of Mounties to pull me off Chip when I get my hands on him.

To Sam, John asked, "Do you think he's doing this alone, or do you think Linette or Chuck have told him to do it?"

Sam raised his hands in a gesture of surrender. "Don't ask me, John. I don't know these people. Linette's only been here once before, and that was to get a property valuation for the cottage. Chuck and Chip? Who on earth gives their kids names like that? Poor guys. No wonder they are so screwed up."

Izzy chortled, "They are derived from Charles and Jean-Pierre, which got shortened to JP, and then finally, Chip."

"Poor guys," Sam said again, shaking his head.

Emma rose from her chair. "I don't know about everyone else, but I have work to do, and this table is where I do it!"

Emma could be very authoritarian when she wanted to be, and she felt this was one day when things needed to be organized by someone with a clear idea of what to do. "John, Izzy, you drive to Sydney in my hatchback and sort out security. While you're there, John, go see Kate and discuss your divorce, separation, whatever."

Then Emma turned her attention to Sam. "Please stay here this morning, Sam, if you can, and handle the detectives when they come to take fingerprints. Fill them in about this conversation and things like that."

Emma looked at them all standing there and then clapped her hands together sharply. "Chop, chop, everyone. The day's not getting any younger."

John had a sports car in the toy hauler section of the motorhome, but the detectives had told him to leave the vehicle exactly as he had found it that morning.

Izzy and John happily squeezed into the hatchback and drove off down the road, waving merrily. They both enjoyed being active.

Sam gave a sigh of relief. "I love your family, Em, but they can be very vocal when they want to be."

Emma laughed when Sam said that. It was lovely to be just the two of them again.

$$\infty \, \infty \, \infty$$

Izzy and John returned to Songbird Cottage the next day. They had decided to concentrate on getting security when they arrived, and then John went to visit Kate the next morning.

They were full of news for Emma when they came back.

Izzy related her story to an interested Sam and Emma first.

It turned out that they had not been the security company's first customers interested in surveillance equipment. When an eager John had made inquiries about a complete home security system installation and round-the-clock surveillance for Songbird Cottage, the security company owner had looked at them in surprise and then commented that they were not the first people asking about cameras for somewhere in Pleasant Bay. He said a man had come into the shop looking to buy a camouflaged camera, one used for wildlife. He said he'd told the man he'd have better luck ordering such a thing online.

"This is where it gets fishy, Mom, because he said the man gave Songbird Cottage as his address, and the owner knew he didn't live here because he's friends with Kate, and Kate had recently told him that a widow was currently staying at the cottage."

Emma couldn't stop herself from saying, "I will design a great website for this store owner if he ever wants one, and I'll do it for free!"

Everyone nodded in agreement.

"The guy was a great help to us, Mom, and he's on his way tomorrow to fix us up with a security and surveillance system even Jason Bourne would have trouble taking out." Izzy looked pleased.

Next, it was John's turn to speak. He kept it short, knowing that Emma would want to get dinner on the stove soon.

"I went to see Kate. She's quite a lady. Really knows her stuff. She says she'll be happy to represent me and asked me to send a courier over with all my paperwork from Gerald." He paused, then said, "why didn't you tell me she was such a looker, Emma? Blonde and baby-blue eyes, quite the knockout."

"Ewww, Dad," Izzy complained, "too soon and *definitely* TMI."

"You're twenty-seven, Izzy, not seven years old. Get over it," was all John said, but he shut up about Kate and started pushing icons on his phone to find Gerald's number.

Sam said nothing and disappeared out the front door quietly while Emma busied herself in the kitchen. Emma figured he was going to wipe the black fingerprint powder off the RV as he had said he would earlier that day.

Emma busied herself with supper. She threw vegetables and stock into a pot, and soon, a delicious aroma filled the cottage.

Sam came back in and approached everyone individually. To each person, he whispered in their ear, "Don't say anything, or react, but follow me outside."

Izzy, John, and Emma looked at each other in surprise, and

then they followed Sam. He was doing something quite extraordinary. He had slid open one of the cottage windows at the side of the cottage and was climbing out of it. All three remaining people followed him.

We must look like a crazy family of monkeys doing this, if anyone were here to see it.

When they got outside, Sam motioned for them all to gather in a circle, and after they had, he began whispering just loud enough for only the three listeners to hear.

"I went outside to check things out because I now know what I'm looking for. There's a hidden camera up in the trees opposite the cottage. It can't see us from here, but I think it might be equipped with ultrasonic listening capabilities, as well as night vision."

Emma was vaguely aware of John's face turning red with rage again and rushed to fill in the angry silence with some good advice.

"No one react. We go back inside and act casual. Talk about normal things."

"You're right, Mom," Izzy whispered, "Ten to one, that thing can listen to us and maybe even track our movements with infrared sensors through the walls."

Sam continued speaking softly. "The heat from the stove and oven, not to mention the fan heater, will confuse any infrared reading capabilities, Izz. I think you should cancel the security installation, John. Better that we say out loud we think it was a random vandal attack, and that we are so happy the pest had his fun and moved on."

"But that eavesdropping jerk, Chip, has heard all our speculation about it being him already!" John hissed.

"I know the online delivery service to and from Cape Breton like the back of my hand, John," Sam whispered, "and I can guarantee you that spy stuff would've only arrived today—yesterday evening at the earliest. Also, the bushes where he stood to get a bead on the best angles are all crushed, and they definitely weren't all flattened like that yesterday afternoon."

Sam gave them all a pat on the back, and they climbed back in through the window.

"Well, that meal smells delicious, Mom," Izzy said loudly with a wink. "I can't wait to eat—I'm starving."

John joined in the game.

"I think I'm overreacting to this silly vandalism. I think I'll cancel the security installation, and we can all get a good night's sleep tonight. Then he moved over to Sam and began to type a message into his phone. When he had finished, he showed the screen to Sam and then Emma.

This is what they read:

Give us blankets and a Thermos of coffee. Sam, will you please stay up with me tonight? Let's see if Chip tries to come back.

Chapter Seven: To Catch a Sneak

The charade continued after dinner. "I think I'll sleep on the sofa tonight, if you don't mind, Emma," John said clearly.

"I'm off to play my apps in bed," Izzy chimed in. "I'm tired too."

"Please stay the night with me up in the mezzanine bedroom, Sam." Emma privately thought they sounded like a bad play for voices from the days when radio was the only form of entertainment.

A chorus of loud "good nights" sounded around the cottage, and a few minutes later, Emma turned off the lights. Sam had stacked the fireplace with heaps of coal and had lit it during dinner. The fire blazed hot and fierce, even though Sam had whispered into Emma's ear, "Infrared cameras are too hi-tech for online spyware stores. I doubt if ol' Chip would have gotten one, but the fire will make Izzy rest easier."

In the dark, Sam and John sneaked back out the window and went to wait in the garden. The night was cool, clear, and crisp.

The occasional hoot of an owl would sound, and Emma would think about the little surveillance team outside and hope they were awake and warm. She also hoped they were having fun. She knew an adventure of some kind was maybe just what John needed to reanimate him. She gradually nodded off to sleep and dreamed of shadowy lurking figures fighting in the dark.

A loud shout woke Emma from a particularly confusing dream. She had gone to bed wearing her sweats and jumped into action immediately.

"Izz!" she shouted downstairs as she hopped from one foot to the other while pulling on her socks. "I think they've got him!"

Izzy bolted out of the bedroom below her, carrying a baseball bat she had dug up out of the girls' old toy chest.

Only stopping briefly to tug on their boots at the door, the two women rushed out into the garden.

The moon was already sinking behind the forest's tree line, and Emma gauged the time to be in the wee hours of the morning, no more than two o'clock. The moonbeams showed her the most welcome sight in Songbird Cottage's front yard. John and Sam were sitting on top of a supine figure lying on the ground. The figure's legs and arms were pummeling and flailing but to no avail. The two men had big grins on their faces, and on one side of the supine heap that was Chip, an upended can of paint could clearly be seen.

"He was trying to throw the contents of that can over the hatchback when we caught him in the act," John said as they got closer. "Sam tackled him to the ground, while I got him doing it on camera." He stopped the telling of his tale so he could glance down and flick Chip's balding head hard using his thumb and middle finger. "Isn't that right, Chippie?"

Chip let out a string of curse words and tried to heave the two men off him.

"Best you stop struggling, buddy," Sam said. "You can stop filming now, John, and call the Mounties over."

Izzy went to bend over and look at Chip with a huge grin on her face. Then she said, "Hold off on making that call a while, Dad. I have a better idea."

"Whatever that idea is, Izzy, can you put it on hold while your father and I get this rogue inside. I think we all deserve a nice cup of tea and to see if that fire is still giving out some warmth," Sam suggested.

The triumphant party went inside, strong-arming the bedraggled Chip with them. Izzy had found a stick on the ground in the garden and walked behind him, poking him with the sharp end every now and again. He would yelp and struggle a bit, but Sam and John had him in an iron grip. John shut the door and the window through which he and Sam had climbed, while Sam pushed Chip firmly down onto the velvet sofa.

Izzy began telling them her idea straight away. "We can use this as a bargaining chip—pun intended."

The tension of the last few hours magically melted away, and everyone in the cottage burst out laughing, everyone except Chip, who continued to stare sullenly at the floor, giving everyone in the room a perfect view of his bald spot.

"Contact Linette—it was her who put you up to this, wasn't it Chippie?—and tell her this one here goes to jail unless she gives you a hassle-free divorce, Dad. What do you think?"

John's eyes lit up, and his face flooded with hope. "That's a brilliant idea, Izz! Why didn't I think of that?"

Emma smiled and said, "She's a daughter after your own heart, John. I think it's the best way to move forward, don't you?"

"Yes," John agreed, "but I still want some answers!" He took a chair from the dining table and positioned himself in front of Chip. "Whose idea was it to terrorize my family, Chip? If you lie, you can look forward to a lengthy legal battle that will have the power to drag you away from your computer games for a very long time, so tell it to me straight, and you never know, I might find it in my heart to make provision for your parasitic existence in my divorce settlement."

Chip tried to sit up straighter on the couch, but its voluminous cushions simply folded him deeper into its depths.

"It was my mom's idea," Chip admitted. "She thought you had hooked up with her again," indicating to where Emma stood with a jerk of his head, "so I came here even before you left to see what was going on."

"Sounds about right," Sam interjected. "That would be around the time Em saw you on Pleasant Bay Road. You didn't recognize the hatchback yet because when you drove by the cottage, Em was still up at the store. That was how she was able to spot you, but you didn't register it was her until you saw the car in the driveway."

"What? I dunno what you mean, man. I was driving around my first day here trying to find a place to stay. Everyone here seems to know each other, and I didn't want anyone talking about me— my surname is very distinguished, you know."

"Oh yeah, Count du Pont," Izzy scoffed, "your surname is so illustrious that one million other folks in the world have it."

Emma knew this kind of bantering would get them nowhere. She turned to Sam and asked, "Honey, please can we use your phone? I think John should call Linette right now and tell her about the situation, and she might not answer if it's a number she recognizes. Can you all go over to the motorhome, please? I want this person out of my house, now. Lock him up in the toy hauler until Linette has agreed to sign the divorce papers. If she proves reluctant, Chip might be in for quite a protracted stay at Songbird Cottage, and he's definitely not doing that here under my roof."

"Up you get, Monsieur du Pont," Sam said as he lifted Chip off the couch by yanking him under the armpits. "I have a feeling your dear mama is not going to be too happy with you, so if I were you, I would encourage her to take whatever deal your stepfather offers her."

The three men left, and Izzy went trailing behind them, still valiantly poking Chip's backside with her stick.

Emma felt exhilarated and knew she would not be able to get back to sleep again that night. As she went upstairs to her little bedroom, she realized her family might finally be free from the dark forces of Linette's toxic influence forever. They had the film of Chip trespassing with intent to vandalize property, so they finally had the bargaining chip Izzy mentioned, which would force Linette to back down and leave them all alone.

Glee surged through Emma's body. It was complete happiness that included a righteous sense of retribution mixed in. Her mind was cast back to the saddest moment in her married life, when she had received a phone call from one of John's friends at work.

"Emma," the friend had said with no polite niceties to soften the blow that was coming, "John is having an affair with a florist who works at a booth downstairs at the Midtown clinic. I think you should know. Her name's Linette du Pont, and she's a bit of a laughingstock with all of us doctors because she's been trying to snap one of us up since even before her husband left her."

Emma remembered how the room had spun in circles around her, and she'd felt nausea rise up into her throat. She recalled perfectly how she had walked to the taxi stand outside their uptown apartment and shakily asked the driver to take her to the clinic.

The trip had been a complete nightmare; tears had been pouring silently down her face, and her chest had heaved up and down as she tried to control her breathing. The cab driver had turned around to her when they halted at a red traffic light, and asked, "You okay, miss?"

Emma had nodded, gulped, and managed to pull herself together long enough to ask the receptionist to call Dr. Havisham to the desk. She'd told Emma the doctor was with a patient, and Emma had walked, as though in a nightmare, straight into the room where John was putting in stitches.

Their eyes had met across the room, and John had known instantly that Emma knew. He had pushed the tray of medical instruments to one side and spoken abruptly to one of the nurses who was standing next to the patient with her mouth open at Emma's unexpected entrance.

And now it's Linette's turn to know what it feels like to have her world turned utterly upside down in one millisecond.

Emma had been wrong. She slept like a baby that night until the sun rose on another beautiful day at Songbird Cottage.

Epilogue

"Mom, guess who Dad's brought with him as his plus-one to the wedding?" Claire was peeping out of Songbird Cottage's now infamous side window, and Emma's memory flashed back to the night when she and Sam had climbed out of it.

Emma was able to see from where she sat at the dining table how her eldest daughter had completely transformed the garden into a fairyland dell filled with multicolored flowers and fronds of green. Underneath the apple tree that spread its branches over the lawn in a benevolent embrace, Claire had set up three trestle tables at right angles to one another. They were covered with white linen tablecloths in preparation for the buffet lunch planned for after the ceremony.

"I'm going to take a wild guess and say Kate," Emma suggested, and Izzy made shushing noises.

Emma closed her lips and her eyes as Isabelle brushed setting powder lightly over her face. "Don't make it too thick, Izz," her mother muttered through her shut mouth, "Enough to control shine, but not so much as to make me look artificially matte."

"Trust me, Mother," Izzy said, "by the time I'm finished, you are going to look like the perfect bride."

Emma smiled inside as her heart was set aglow at the thought of whom she was marrying on this glorious Cape Breton summer's day. Summertime was drawing to a close, and some of the leaves had even begun to change hue from verdant green to mellow yellows, oranges, and russet reds. The weather was still warm enough for the cottage roof to creak and crackle as it stretched underneath the sunshine.

Claire turned away from the window and began to reapply her lip balm with the little finger of her right hand. Emma wasn't able to see that Claire's expression was melancholy because Izzy was brushing eyeshadow over her eyelids. Even if she had caught a glimpse of Claire's sad expression, she might have guessed it was because her eldest daughter was upset her boyfriend Giulio had had to stay in Bangor, Maine and couldn't accompany her to the wedding. She'd given no explanation about his absence, and Emma knew her daughter well enough to realize she would open up about it when the time was right.

"There, you're all finished." Isabelle sat back to admire her work from a distance. There was a knock on the door, and John walked in after hearing Izzy's command to enter. He stopped at the open door for one second to appreciate the beautiful tableau his ex-wife and two daughters made as they all sat together on one of the beds in Claire and Izzy's old room. He gave a nostalgic smile as he saw the baseball bat Izzy used to carry around everywhere with her when she was little.

"Well," he said to Emma as he came closer into the room, "are you ready to say goodbye to Songbird Cottage?"

Emma thought a bit before simply blurting out the first thing that came into her mind.

Am I ready to leave Songbird Cottage and go to live across the way? It might only be a couple of hundred yards, but the move means much more than a measurement of distance.

Emma had lived here at the cottage for nearly one year. She had arrived in a wretched state of misery and mistrust, and now here she was, preparing to wed the man she should have married eighteen years ago.

Maybe fickle fate had been right to tear me and Sam apart all those years ago. Maybe I still had some growing up to do.

Emma looked across the room at John with deep fondness in her eyes.

"Yes, John," she said, "I'm ready to leave the cottage, but not the sunshine and songbirds. They'll be following me to the brewery."

"Hey, it's not all songbirds and sunshine, you know," John said. "Into every life, a little rain—and a whole lot of Canadian snow—must fall!"

The three women laughed.

"The winters are part of the beauty of this place, Dad," Claire said as she helped her mother put on her low-slung shoes. "Mom sent me pics when she was here during winter, and I found them fascinating. I don't know why we only ever came here in summer. You know the sun is so bad for my skin." Claire swung back a swath of her long, red hair.

"I'll be able to tell you about my impressions of what winters are like in Cape Breton this year," John promised. "I'm going to be spending a lot of time between here and Sydney, with Kate." When every eye in the room swung around to look at him, John held up his hands in a go-slow gesture. "I mean that Kate and I are going to be finalizing my divorce from Linette."

Izzy nudged her sister in the ribs. "Hoy! I saw that, young lady," John said with a grin.

He turned to Emma, "Are you ready?"

Emma gave herself one last look in the mirror, then she went to hug Izzy. "Thank you, my darling," she said. "My dress is wonderful." Then she went to give Claire a hug. "Thank you too, my dearest girl, for such a lovely reception area."

Emma went to stand beside John and looped her arm through his.

"Third time's the charm?" Emma asked, full of hope as she smiled at him.

In all seriousness, John responded, "Emma, I treated you badly and threw away our marriage and our family to be with someone who wasn't worth it. Can you forgive me for being so cruel and blind for so many years?"

Emma knew she had truly forgiven John when she looked inside her soul.

"Yes, John. I can. I already have."

John nodded, and they walked out of the room, out of Songbird Cottage, and Emma only stopped when John had let her go to take her rightful place by Sam's side.

∞ ∞ ∞

Continue the story with *Escape to Songbird Cottage* (Pleasant Bay Book 3).

Thank you, readers!

Thank you for reading this book. It is important to me to share my stories with you and that you enjoy them. May I ask of you a favor? If you enjoyed this book, will you please take a moment to leave a review on Amazon and/or Goodreads? Thank you for your support!

Also, each week, I send my readers updates about my life as well as information about my new releases, freebies, promos, and book recommendations. If you're interested in receiving my weekly newsletter, please go to newsletter.sylviaprice.com, and it will ask you for your email. As a thank-you, you will receive a FREE exclusive short story that isn't available for purchase!

Blessings,
Sylvia

Escape to
Songbird
Cottage
BOOK THREE
A PLEASANT BAY
NOVEL
SYLVIA PRICE

Songbird Cottage Beginnings

Get it for FREE!

Sam MacAuley and his wife Annalize are total opposites. When Sam wants to leave city life in Halifax to get a plot of land on Cape Breton Island, where he grew up, his wife wants nothing to do with his plans and opts to move herself and their three boys back to her home country of South Africa.

As Sam settles into a new life on his own, his friend Lachlan encourages him to get back into the dating scene. Although he meets plenty of women, he longs to find the one with whom he wants to share the rest of his life. Will Sam ever meet "the one"?

The Songbird Cottage (Pleasant Bay Book 1)

Emma Copeland and her daughters, Claire and Isabelle, spend their summers at Songbird Cottage in Pleasant Bay, Nova Scotia. While there, Emma enjoys the company of her ruggedly handsome neighbor, Sam MacAuley, but when something happens between them, she vows never to return to Songbird Cottage.

When Emma turns fifty, she rushes into a marriage with smooth-talking Andrew Schönfeld, but when he suddenly dies, Emma loses everything.

With her life in shambles, and with nowhere else to stay, Emma returns to Songbird Cottage. Despite leaving without an explanation eighteen years ago, Sam is quick to Emma's aid when she arrives on Cape Breton.

As the beauty and peacefulness of Pleasant Bay begin to heal Emma, she gets some shocking news, and she discovers that she's unwelcomed at Songbird Cottage. Will she be able to piece her life back together and get another chance at happiness?

Escape To Songbird Cottage (Pleasant Bay Book 3)

Emma Copeland's eldest daughter, Claire, is finally getting married. At thirty-two, Claire is about to wed her long-time boyfriend, Guilio Bondi, and she should be ecstatic, but she isn't. Deciding that she had better get out of the relationship before she's roped into an unhappy marriage, Claire escapes to her father's summer home at Pleasant Bay, just down the road from her mother.

While staying at Songbird Cottage, Claire meets Richard Benson, a handsome lawyer who has moved back to the island to care for his ailing mother. Richard is mature and thoughtful, everything Guilio isn't. But will Guilio let Claire go that easily?

Secrets Of Songbird Cottage (Pleasant Bay Book 4)

Claire Havisham is enjoying her first winter at Songbird Cottage. As her relationship with her boyfriend, Richard Benson, is warming up, they discover that they've both been keeping secrets from each other.

Claire has been receiving gifts and packages from a secret admirer, but she doesn't want anyone to know. Richard, who had left Montreal to move back home to Cape Breton Island to help care for his ailing mother, drops a bombshell on Claire when he announces that his fiancée, Geneviève Allaire, has arrived in town. Can Claire and Richard's relationship survive these secrets?

Seasons At Songbird Cottage (Pleasant Bay Book 5)

Emma Copeland's family and friends are gathering at Songbird Cottage for a special celebration in honor of her eldest daughter, Claire. Everyone, except for Emma's youngest daughter Isabelle, is excited to see each other again. Izzy was an aspiring musician, but since her band broke up, her life has been in a downward spiral. Her self-destructive behavior worries Emma and Claire, but they are at a loss as to what to do when Izzy runs back to New York.

With no one in her family able to help her, Emma's husband, Sam, sends his youngest son Luke, a childhood friend of Izzy's, to bring her back to Songbird Cottage. The cottage had been a place of healing for both Emma and Claire. Will Izzy accept Luke's help and let Songbird Cottage work its magic?

Jonah's Redemption: Book 1 (An Amish Romance)

FREE ON AMAZON!

Jonah has lost his community, and he's struggling to get by in the English world. He yearns for his Amish roots, but his past mistakes keep him from returning home.

Mary Lou is recovering from a medical scare. Her journey has impressed upon her how precious life is, so she decides to go on rumspringa to see the world.

While in the city, Mary Lou meets Jonah. Unable to understand his foul attitude, especially towards her, she makes every effort to share her faith with him. As she helps him heal from his past, an attraction develops.

Will Jonah's heart soften towards Mary Lou? What will God do with these two broken people?

Jonah's Redemption: Boxed Set (An Amish Romance)

If you loved Jonah's Redemption: Book 1 (available for free on Amazon), grab the rest of the series in this special boxed set featuring Books 2-5, plus a bonus epilogue and companion story.

Mary Lou's fiancé leaves her as soon as tragedy strikes. Unwilling to resent him, she chooses, instead, to find him. Her misfortunes pile up in her quest to return Jonah to the Amish faith, but she is undeterred, for God has given her a mission.

Will Mary Lou's faith be enough to help them get through the countless obstacles that are thrown their way? Do Jonah and Mary Lou have a chance at happiness?

Join Jonah and Mary Lou as they wrestle with love, a life worth living, and their unique faith in Christ. Enjoy the conclusion of Jonah's Redemption in this exclusive boxed set, with a bonus epilogue and companion story!

The Christmas Arrival: An Amish Holiday Romance

Rachel Lapp is a young Amish woman who is the daughter of the community's bishop. She is in the midst of planning the annual Christmas Nativity play when newcomer Noah Miller arrives in town to spend Christmas with his cousins. Encouraged by her father to welcome the new arrival, Rachel asks Noah to be a part of the Nativity.

Despite Rachel's engagement to Samuel King, a local farmer, she finds herself irrevocably drawn to Noah and his carefree spirit. Reserved and slightly shy, Noah is hesitant to get involved in the play, but an unlikely friendship begins to develop between Rachel and Noah, bringing with it unexpected problems, including a seemingly harmless prank with life-threatening consequences that require a Christmas miracle.

Will Rachel honor her commitment to Samuel, or will Noah win her affections?

Join these characters on what is sure to be a heartwarming holiday adventure! Instead of waiting for each part to be released, enjoy the entire Christmas Arrival series in this exclusive collection!

About the Author

Sylvia Price

Now an Amazon bestselling author, Sylvia Price is an author of Amish and contemporary romance and women's fiction. She especially loves writing uplifting stories about second chances!

Although raised in the cosmopolitan city of Montréal, Sylvia spent her adolescent and young adult years in Nova Scotia, and the beautiful countryside landscapes and ocean views serve as the backdrop to her contemporary novels.

After meeting and falling in love with an American while living abroad, Sylvia now resides in the US. She spends her days writing, hoping to inspire the next generation to read more stories. When she's not writing, Sylvia stays busy making sure her three young children are alive and well-fed.

Subscribe to Sylvia's newsletter at newsletter.sylviaprice.com to stay in the loop about new releases, freebies, promos, and more. As a thank-you, you will receive a FREE exclusive short story that isn't available for purchase.

Learn more about Sylvia at amazon.com/author/sylviaprice and goodreads.com/author/show/1134593.Sylvia_Price.

Follow Sylvia on Facebook at facebook.com/sylviapriceauthor for updates.

Join Sylvia's Advanced Reader Copies (ARC) team at arcteam.sylviaprice.com to get her books for free before they are released in exchange for honest reviews.